Note to parents, carers and teachers

Read it yourself is a series of modern stories, favourite characters and traditional tales written in a simple way for children who are learning to read. The books can be read independently or as part of a guided reading session.

Each book is carefully structured to include many high-frequency words vital for first reading. The sentences on each page are supported closely by pictures to help with understanding, and to offer lively details to talk about.

The books are graded into four levels that progressively introduce wider vocabulary and longer stories as a reader's ability and confidence grows.

Ideas for use

- Begin by looking through the book and talking about the pictures. Has your child heard this story before?

- Help your child with any words he does not know, either by helping him to sound them out or supplying them yourself.

- Developing readers can be concentrating so hard on the words that they sometimes don't fully grasp the meaning of what they're reading. Answering the puzzle questions on pages 30 and 31 will help with understanding.

For more information and advice on Read it yourself and book banding, visit **www.ladybird.com/readityourself**

Book
Band
4

Level 1 is ideal for children who have received some initial reading instruction. Each story is told very simply, using a small number of frequently repeated words.

Special features:

The old woman

The old man

The boy

The girl

The dog

The enormous turnip

6

7

Opening pages introduce key story words

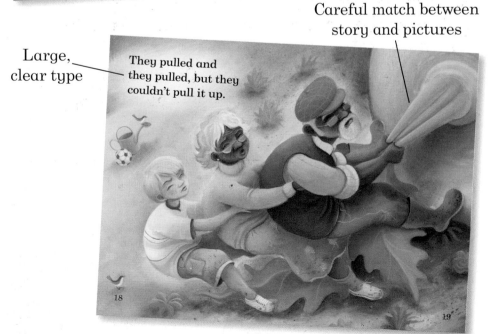

Careful match between story and pictures

Large, clear type

They pulled and they pulled, but they couldn't pull it up.

18

19

Educational Consultant: Geraldine Taylor
Book Banding Consultant: Kate Ruttle

A catalogue record for this book is available from the British Library

Published by Ladybird Books Ltd
80 Strand, London, WC2R 0RL
A Penguin Company

005

ISBN: 978-0-72327-278-6

Printed in China

The Enormous Turnip

Illustrated by Richard Johnson

The old man

The enormous turnip

The old woman

The boy

The girl

The dog

The old man planted some turnip seeds.

The turnip seeds grew and grew.

One turnip grew enormous.

"I want that enormous turnip for my tea," said the old man.

He pulled and he pulled, but he couldn't pull it up.

The old man called
to the old woman.

"Help me pull up this
enormous turnip,"
he said.

They pulled and
they pulled, but they
couldn't pull it up.

15

The old woman
called to the boy.

"Help us pull up this
enormous turnip,"
she said.

They pulled and
they pulled, but they
couldn't pull it up.

19

The boy called
to the girl.

"Help us pull up
this enormous
turnip," he said.

They pulled and
they pulled, but they
couldn't pull it up.

The girl called to the dog.

"Help us pull up this enormous turnip," she said.

They pulled and
they pulled and
they pulled.

Up popped the
enormous turnip!

27

And they all had turnip for tea.

How much do you remember about the story of The Enormous Turnip? Answer these questions and find out!

- **What does the old man plant?**

  A enormous turnip, A enormous turnip.

- **Who does the old man ask to help him pull up the enormous turnip?**

  The old woman The old wooman

- **Who does the girl ask to help her pull up the enormous turnip?**

  The dog The dog

Look at the pictures from the story and say the order they should go in.

Read it yourself with Ladybird

Tick the books you've read!

For children who are ready to take their first steps in reading

Level 1

The Enormous Turnip

Fairy Friends

Goldilocks and the Three Bears

Little Red Hen

The Magic Porridge Pot

Little Creatures

Recycling Fun!

The Princess and the Pea

Cinderella

Rex the Big Dinosaur

The Tale of Peter Rabbit

The Three Billy Goats Gruff

Why Giraffe has a Long Neck

Topsy and Tim Go to the Zoo

The Ugly Duckling

The Emperor's New Clothes

For beginner readers who can read short, simple sentences with help.

Level 2

Beauty and the Beast

Chicken Licken

Little Red Riding Hood

Nature Trail

Sports Day

Pirate School

Rumpelstiltskin

Sleeping Beauty

The Gingerbread Man

Sly Fox and Red Hen

The Tale of Jemima Puddle-Duck

The Three Little Pigs

Why Lion ROARRRS!

Topsy and Tim The Big Race

Town Mouse and Country Mouse

Dom's Dragon

Available on the App Store

The Read it yourself with Ladybird app is now available for iPad, iPhone and iPod touch

App also available on Android devices